Weekly Reader Books presents

Don't Be My Valentine

Joan M. Lexau

pictures by Syd Hoff

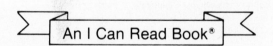
An I Can Read Book®

Harper & Row, Publishers

This book is a presentation of Weekly Reader Books.
Weekly Reader Books offers book clubs for children
from preschool through high school. For further
information write to: **Weekly Reader Books,**
4343 Equity Drive, Columbus, Ohio 43228.

Published by arrangement with Harper & Row, Publishers, Inc.
Weekly Reader is a trademark of Field Publications.
I Can Read Book is a registered trademark of
Harper & Row, Publishers, Inc.

Library of Congress Cataloging in Publication Data
Lexau, Joan M.
    Don't be my valentine.

    (An I can read book)
    Summary: Sam's mean valentine for Amy Lou goes
astray at school and almost ruins the day for him
and his friends.
    1. Children's stories, American. [1. Valentines—
Fiction. 2. Valentine's Day—Fiction. 3. Friendship—
Fiction. 4. Schools—Fiction] I. Hoff, Syd,
1912–   ill. II. Title. III. Series.
PZ7.L5895Dp 1985   [E]   85-42621
ISBN 0-06-023872-0
ISBN 0-06-023873-9 (lib. bdg.)

Don't Be
My Valentine

"Tomorrow is Valentine's Day,"

Mrs. Plum said,

"so today we will make valentines.

Take out a sheet of red paper."

5

Sam took out a sheet of red paper.

"Fold it in half," Mrs. Plum said.

Sam folded his paper in half.

6

"Begin on the fold,"

the teacher said.

"Now draw a line

like a big fish hook."

7

Amy Lou turned around and said,

"I will help you, Sam."

"I can do it," Sam said.

"Amy Lou," Mrs. Plum said,

"you do your own work.

Let Sam do his."

Sam drew a big fish hook.

"Now cut around the fish hook,"

the teacher said.

"Then open up the paper,

and you have a valentine heart."

Sam cut around the fish hook.

Then he opened his paper.

It was in two pieces.

10

Before he could hide them,

Amy Lou saw them.

"You did it wrong," she said.

"You didn't begin on the fold."

Sam said, "I did it wrong

because you were bugging me."

"I only wanted to help,"

Amy Lou said.

"Who asked you to?" Sam yelled.

"Now, now," the teacher said.

"It will be all right."

She took some tape

and taped Sam's valentine together.

Mrs. Plum wrote on the board,

Roses are red.

Violets are blue.

I like to go

to school with you.

I want U 4 my valentine.

She drew flowers all around it.

"You can use this," she said,

"or you can make up your own."

Amy Lou whispered to Sam,

"I will show you

how to draw flowers on it.

Then you can send it to me."

"Don't bug me, Amy Lou," Sam said.

"Why would I send one to you?"

"Sam," the teacher said,

"this is not talking time."

Sam wanted to tell Mrs. Plum

that Amy Lou talked to him first.

But Amy Lou was working

on her valentine.

She looked very busy.

Sam wrote on his valentine,

Roses are red.

Violets are blue.

He wanted to make up

his own valentine.

"What goes with blue?"

he asked himself.

Sam looked at Amy Lou's back

and smiled.

A good idea came to him.

He wrote,

How did you ever

get out of the zoo?

DON'T BE MY VALENTINE.

From Sam.

He drew a monkey on it.

17

The bell rang.

Everyone ran to get their coats.

The teacher said, "Amy Lou and Sam,

don't forget the cookies

for our valentine party."

Sam reached into his coat pocket.

There was the note

the teacher had given him

to give to his parents.

"Oh, no!" Sam said to himself.

"I forgot all about it."

19

"Tomorrow," Mrs. Plum said,

"bring valentines for everybody

so everyone will get

the same number."

Amy Lou looked at Sam and said,

"Now you *have* to send me

a valentine."

Sam stuck out his tongue at her.

He put the valentine he had made

in his coat pocket.

"Come on, let's run home
and get away from Amy Lou,"
Sam said to his friend Albert.
"I have to go to the dentist,"
Albert said.

"See you tomorrow,"

Sam said.

He ran all the way home.

Sam's father had bought valentines
for Sam to send.

He helped Sam put names on them.

"Pick out nice ones for your teacher

and Albert and Amy Lou,"

his father said.

"I *made* one for Amy Lou," Sam said.

"That's nice," his father said.

In the morning Albert was waiting

for Sam on the corner.

Sam said,

"I made a valentine for Amy Lou."

He reached into his pocket

and pulled out the cookie note.

"Oh, no!" Sam said.

"I forgot about the cookies!"

Sam showed Albert

the valentine he had made.

"I have to put

Amy Lou's name on it.

I will do that at school."

Albert laughed at the card.

"Will Amy Lou be mad at you!"

"Then maybe she will leave me alone,"

Sam said.

"Look out, here she comes!"

Sam and Albert ran to school.

They hung up their coats.

Sam took the cookie note

out of his pocket.

"I guess I should tell Mrs. Plum

about the cookies," he said.

But the teacher was busy.

Sam sat at his desk and waited.

Amy Lou put a big bag

on the teacher's desk.

"I brought chocolate chip,"

she told her friend Gladys.

"What kind of cookies

did you bring, Sam?" Gladys asked.

Sam did not answer.

"You forgot, didn't you?"

Amy Lou said.

"You make me so mad, Amy Lou.

That's why I forget things,"

Sam said.

"You are mean to me,

but I don't forget,"

Amy Lou said.

33

"Class, put your valentines

in this red box," the teacher said.

"We will give them out

at the party this afternoon."

34

"I left Amy Lou's valentine

in my coat," Sam told Albert.

"I still have to put her name on it."

Sam and Albert

ran back to the coat room.

"It's gone!" said Sam.

"Maybe it fell out

when you took out the cookie note,"

Albert said.

They looked all over the floor,

but the valentine was not anywhere.

"Time to sit down,"

the teacher said.

Sam and Albert went back

to their desks.

"I brought lots of cookies,"

Amy Lou said.

"I will tell Mrs. Plum

some of them are from you, Sam.

But I still think you are mean."

She turned back to her desk.

"Thanks, Amy Lou,"

Sam said to her back.

He was glad he had not sent

that mean valentine to her.

She was not so bad sometimes.

The party began after lunch.

"We need two mailmen

to hand out the valentines,"

Mrs. Plum said.

All the children raised their hands.

Amy Lou waved her arm and yelled,

"Me! Me! Me!"

Sam said to her,

"You always think

you should do everything."

Amy Lou gave him a funny look.

She put her hand down.

The teacher picked

Albert and Gladys.

Gladys read out the names.

Albert handed out the valentines.

"Here is one for Sam from Amy Lou,"

Gladys said.

It was a store valentine.

There was a deer on it.

It said,

  You are a deer

  to be my valentine.

  From Amy Lou.

"Thanks, Amy Lou," Sam said.

Gladys said, "Here is a card

for Amy Lou from Sam."

"WHAT!" shouted Sam.

He grabbed the card from Gladys.

It was a store card

with a bear on it.

It said,

I can't bear it

if you won't be my valentine.

From Sam.

Sam *knew* he had not sent a card

to Amy Lou.

"Thank you for the card, Sam.

Now give it to me!"

said Amy Lou.

Sam gave her the card.

45

Mrs. Plum said,

"Sam, I like your card

with the lion on it.

But I do not like the one

you made about the zoo."

"About…about…about…" said Sam.

46

How did Mrs. Plum get the card

he had made for Amy Lou?

"But I didn't send it!" Sam said.

"Didn't you make the card

about the zoo?"

the teacher asked.

"Your name is on it, Sam."

"I did, but I didn't!"

shouted Sam.

The teacher said,

"You did, but you didn't, Sam?"

"Sam made the card,

but he did not make it for you,"

Albert said.

"And he lost it."

48

"YOU did it!" Sam yelled at Albert.

"You were the only one

I told about it.

I bet you sent that other card

to Amy Lou, too.

It isn't funny, Albert."

Sam got up and gave Albert a push.

Albert got up and pushed him back.

"I didn't do it!" Albert yelled.

Amy Lou said,

"Sam, don't be mad at Albert.

If you lost the card,

anyone could have found it."

Sam hoped he was having a bad dream.

Everyone was looking at him.

Albert made a face at him.

"I will get you, Albert!" Sam said.

Sam got up.

Albert ran out of the room.

Sam chased him

down the hall.

"Sam, Albert! Come back!"

the teacher called.

They kept right on running.

"Amy Lou, where are you going?"

the teacher called.

Amy Lou was running

after Sam and Albert.

Albert and Sam and Amy Lou

ran up the stairs to the third floor.

They were too tired to run any more.

"If you were really my friend,"

Sam said to Albert,

"you would not do such a mean thing."

Albert said,

"I never would have sent

your valentine to Mrs. Plum.

Not in a million years!"

"See?" Amy Lou said.

"Albert did not do it."

"Well, somebody did it!" Sam said.

"Sam, you can't even draw,"

Amy Lou said.

"Monkeys do not have ears

like the ones you made."

"When did you see it?" Sam yelled.

"YOU found that card, didn't you?"

"You told me

you would not send me one,"

Amy Lou said.

"So I sent a card from you to me.

Then I found the card you made.

It was really mean,

so I knew it was for me."

"Well, it was even meaner

to send it to the teacher,"

Sam said.

"I know," said Amy Lou.

"That is why

I wanted to be a mailman.

I wanted to get it back."

"Why do you keep saying

I'm mean?" Sam asked.

"I'm not mean."

"You make faces at me,

and you say mean things

when I try to help you,"

Amy Lou said.

"But I do not want you to help me!"

Sam told her.

59

"Sam," Albert said,

"you stop being mean to Amy Lou.

Amy Lou, you stop bugging Sam.

Okay?"

"Okay," Amy Lou said.

"Okay," Sam said,

"and I'm sorry

I did not believe you, Albert."

"We better go back," Albert said.

They ran down to their room.

"Amy Lou," Sam said,

"don't forget to tell Mrs. Plum

the cookies are from me, too."

"That would be helping you,"

Amy Lou said.

"Oh!" Sam said. "I forgot!"

Sam went up to the teacher.

"I forgot to bring cookies.

I'm sorry, Mrs. Plum," he said.

Amy Lou said, "I'm sorry

I sent you that valentine, Mrs. Plum."

Sam said, "I'm sorry

I was mean, Amy Lou."

Amy Lou said, "I'm sorry

I bugged you, Sam."

Mrs. Plum said, "Sam,

you can bring cookies next time."

"I will help you remember, Sam,"

Amy Lou said.

"DO NOT HELP ME, AMY LOU!"

Sam yelled.

"There you go, being mean again!"

said Amy Lou.

"Oh, nuts!" Albert said.

"Here we go again!"